The Flamingo
Who Forgot

First published 2007
Evans Brothers Limited
2A Portman Mansions
Chiltern Street
London W1U 6NR

British Library Cataloguing in Publication Data

Durant, Alan, 1958-
   The flamingo who forgot. - (Spirals)
   1. Children's stories
   I. Title
   823.9'2[J]

ISBN-13: 9780237533496 (HB)
ISBN-13: 9780237533434 (PB)

Printed in China

Series Editor: Nick Turpin
Design: Robert Walster
Production: Jenny Mulvanny

The Flamingo Who Forgot

Alan Durant
and Franco Rivolli

Evans

The flamingo stood in
the lake on one leg.

Along trumped an elephant.

'Why are you standing on one leg?' he asked.

'So that I don't forget,' said the flamingo.

'Elephants never forget,' said the elephant. 'What are you trying to remember?'

The flamingo frowned. 'I've forgotten,' she said.

'Oh, well perhaps I can help,' said the elephant. 'It's bath day today, you know. Perhaps that's what you wanted to remember.' He squirted water into the air.

The flamingo shook her head. 'I bathe everyday,' she said. 'That's not what I've forgotten. But thanks for your help.'

A monkey waltzed by.

'Say, why are you standing like that?' he asked.

'To remember something,' said the flamingo. 'But I've forgotten what.'

'Well, isn't that crazy?' said the monkey. 'But don't worry, I can help. It's the Jungle Dance Contest today. That's what you wanted to remember.'

The flamingo shook her head. 'Flamingos don't dance,' she said. 'That's not what I've forgotten. But thanks for your help.'

Just then a cockatoo flew by.
'Hey. Don't you look funny,' she said.
'I'm trying to remember something
important,' said the flamingo again.
'But I've forgotten what.'

The cockatoo chuckled. 'I can help you there,' she said. 'It's national nest-building day. That's what you're trying to remember.' The cockatoo picked up some twigs and flew up into a tree.

The flamingo shook her head. 'I live in the water and my nest is made of mud,' she said. 'That's not what I've forgotten. But thanks for your help.'

A hyena was the next to stop by.
But he was no help at all. All he did
was laugh and laugh – and the poor
flamingo went pinker than ever.

A fish popped up from under the water.

'Are you the finishing post?' he asked.

'No,' said the flamingo. 'I'm standing on one leg like this to remember something important. But I've forgotten what.'

'Oh,' said the fish with a flick-flack-swish. 'Today's the Lake Swimming Gala. I expect you were trying to remember that.'

The flamingo shook her head. 'I can't swim,' she said. 'I'm sure that's not what I've forgotten. But thanks for your help.'

The flamingo stood in the lake
on one leg, feeling very silly for
being so forgetful.

Along came another flamingo, carrying a parcel.

'Hello, Fedora,' he said. 'I see you're trying to remember something.'

'That's right, Fred,' she sighed. 'But I've forgotten what.'

Fred smiled. 'Perhaps I can help,' he said and he handed Fedora the parcel.

'For me?' she said.

'For you,' said Fred.

Suddenly Fedora smiled so much she went bright pink with happiness.

'At last I've remembered!' she cried – and she put her leg down. 'What I wanted to remember is that today's...

... my birthday!'

'Happy birthday!' said Fred.

Then Fedora the flamingo
had a birthday that she would
never forget!

Why not try reading a Spirals book?

Megan's Tick Tock Rocket by Andrew Fusek Peters,
Polly Peters, and Simona Dimitri
ISBN 978 0237 53342 7

Growl! by Vivian French and Tim Archbold
ISBN 978 0237 53345 8

John and the River Monster by Paul Harrison
and Ian Benfold Haywood
ISBN 978 0237 53344 1

Froggy Went a Hopping by Alan Durant and Sue Mason
ISBN 978 0237 53346 5

Glub! By Penny Little and Sue Mason
ISBN 978 0237 53461 5

Amy's Slippers by Mary Wilkinson and Simona Dimitri
ISBN 978 0237 53347 2

The Grumpy Queen by Valerie Wilding
and Simona Sanfilippo
ISBN 978 0237 53459 2

The Flamingo Who Forgot by Alan Durant
and Franco Rivolli
ISBN 978 0237 53343 4